THiNK BUT A THOUGHT!

JENNIFER ELLEN PARKER

ILLUSTRATED BY ROGER L. MORIN

Think Happy Thoughts!

Jennifer Ellen Parker

Dream "WICKED" Big!

Roger L. Morin

outskirts press

Outskirts Press, Inc.
http://www.outskirtspress.com

Paperback ISBN: 978-1-9772-3630-2
Hardback ISBN: 978-1-9772-3631-9

Cover and illustrations by Roger L. Morin

Outskirts Press and the "OP" logo are trademarks belonging to Outskirts Press, Inc.

PRINTED IN THE UNITED STATES OF AMERICA

This story is dedicated to all of our teachers who have lifted, inspired, and shown us how to be thinkers, dreamers, and innovators!

To Mr. Hood who not only taught us, but knew when it was more important to listen.

To Roger Fuller whose innate ability to affect prose and imagery gave me the confidence to publish my vision.

To all of you who not only thought we could, but knew we would, this book is for you.

Jump in! Hold tight!

I'm woven thick and strong

My basket is yours, to travel far and beyond

Fill fast with whim

Watch balloons paint the sky

Letting go of your worries as we soar so high

Be light, be bold

Float over golden floors

Past green eared pines, sun drenched seas and Maine's rocky shores

Up we shall go

Hold our breath as we climb

Anticipation grows wild like low spreading Thyme

Whirl through tree tops

On the wings of a bird

We sing with the mountains while not speaking a word

Move through time

Visit Giza, Stonehenge

And Taj Mahal, vowing you will
return again

Tip of your hat

As we pass, quick as a mouse

Eiffel Tower, Golden Gate Bridge, and
Sydney Opera House

Time stops, we rise
The two hands move no more
Only heartbeats are heard over our heedful roar

Tromp like giants
Dance with fairies and sprites
Let laughter spill over and frolic
through the night

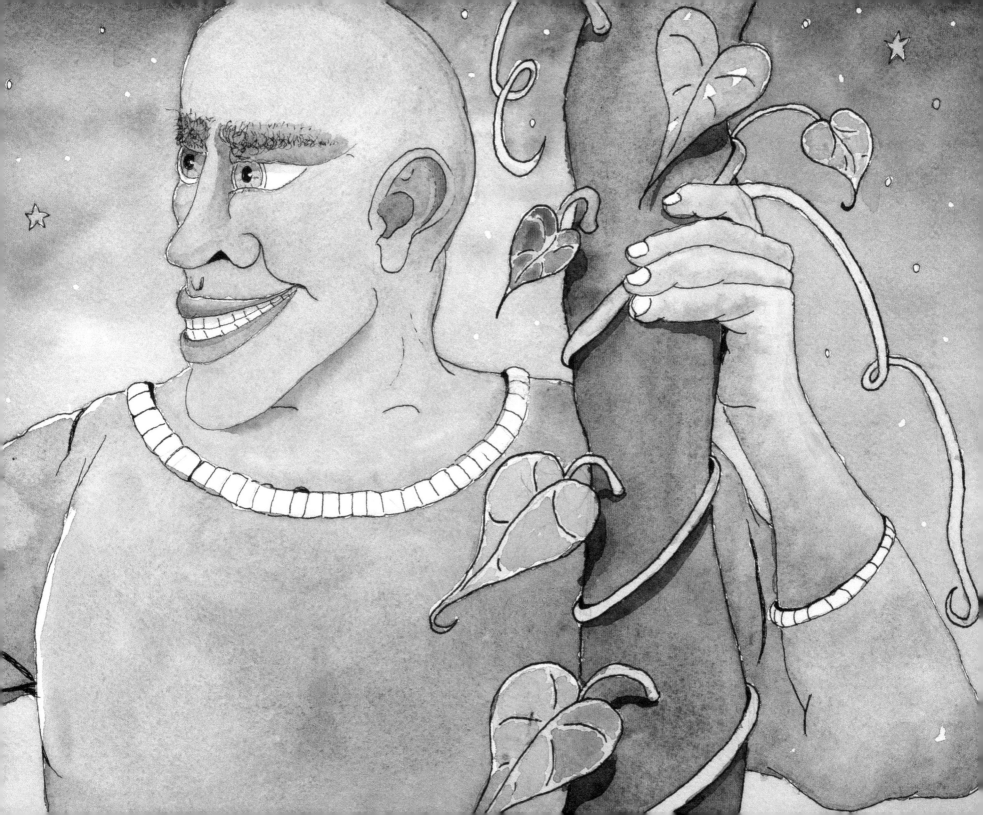

Think but a thought

Let it swirl and be made

For you are the ringmaster and I am the same

Hocus Pocus

Speak your heart's spell

Watch things magically
transform and make all well

Trust me, it's real

You've watched with your own eye

As the moon branches out across the fearless sky

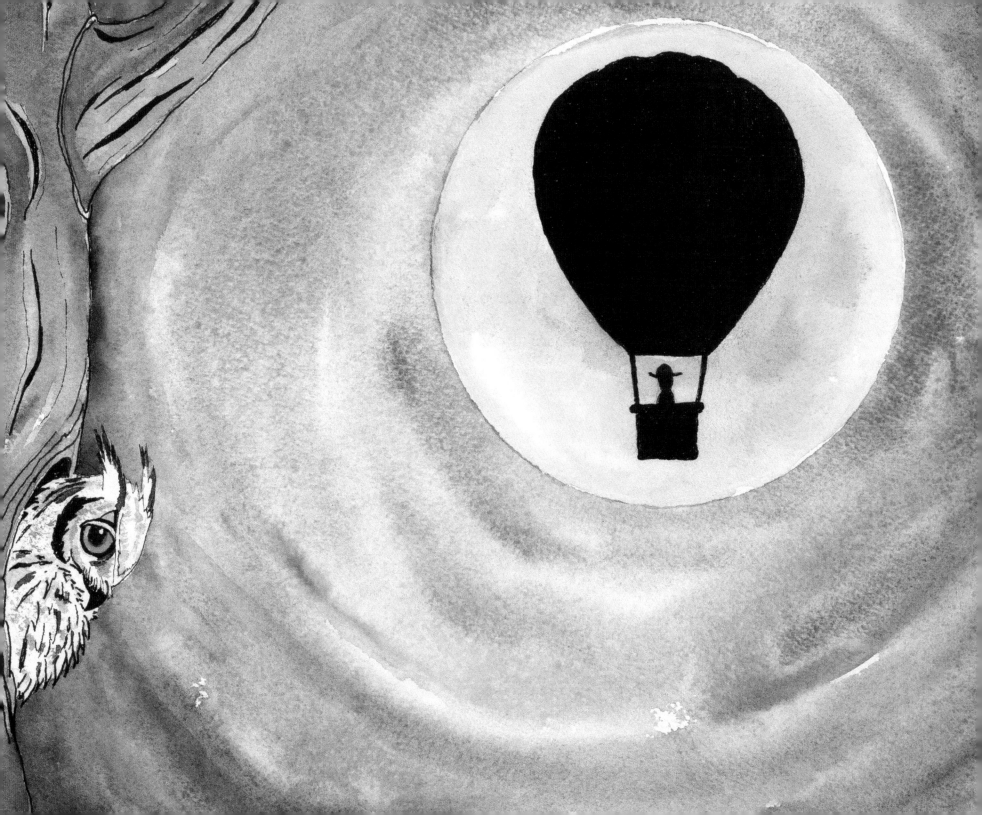

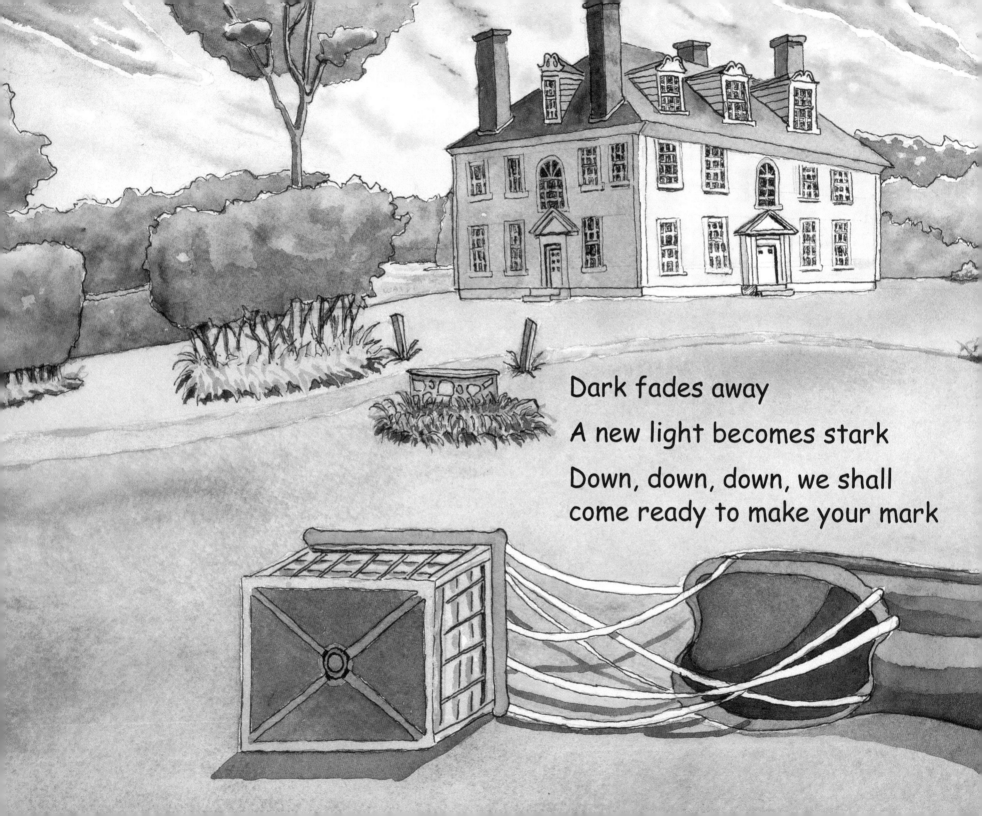

Dark fades away

A new light becomes stark

Down, down, down, we shall
come ready to make your mark

Land your head down

On a pillow of plume

Fall deep into slumber with
dreams ready to bloom

Goodbye for now

Till you call out my name

Adventures are endless; our time together the same

CPSIA information can be obtained at www.ICGtesting.com
Printed in the USA
BVIW120021150221
600114BV00001BA/1